MW00892010

LifeRich Publishing is a registered trademark of The Reader's Digest Association, Inc.

LifeRich Publishing books may be ordered through booksellers or by contacting:

LifeRich Publishing
1663 Liberty Drive
Bloomington, IN 47403
www.liferichpublishing.com
844-686-9607

Because of the dynamic nature of the Internet, any web addresses or links contained in this book may have changed since publication and may no longer be valid. The views expressed in this work are solely those of the author and do not necessarily reflect the views of the publisher, and the publisher hereby disclaims any responsibility for them.

Any people depicted in stock imagery provided by Getty Images are models, and such images are being used for illustrative purposes only.
Certain stock imagery © Getty Images.

Author's photograph courtesy of Karen Tucker

Scripture quotations are from the Holy Bible, King James Version (Authorized Version). First published in 1611. Quoted from the KJV Classic Reference Bible, Copyright © 1983 by The Zondervan Corporation.

Interior Image Credit: David Anthony Jones (not including stock art)

ISBN: 978-1-4897-4420-3 (sc)
ISBN: 978-1-4897-4419-7 (hc)
ISBN: 978-1-4897-4421-0 (e)

Library of Congress Control Number: 2022917387

Print information available on the last page.

LifeRich Publishing rev. date: 10/13/2022

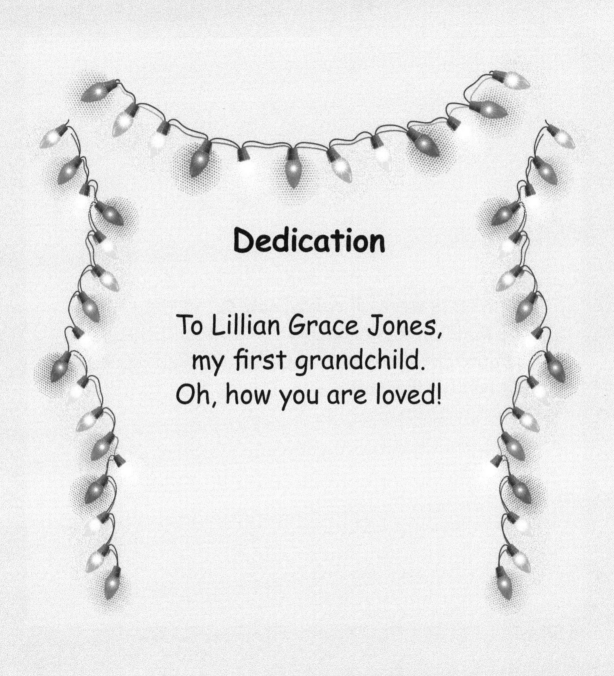

Dedication

To Lillian Grace Jones,
my first grandchild.
Oh, how you are loved!

The gifts were all ready, now set in the sleigh,
and Rudolph was prancing for he'd lead the way.
Santa checked once, then he checked again.
He had his list and a map. It was time to begin.

Before he boarded his timeless old sleigh,
he went to his workshop and started to pray.
He knelt down to the floor with red suit and all,
then took off his cap from his head, nearly bald.

"Jesus," Santa started in a most humble way,
"I bow down before You and just want to say
thank You for letting me care for children of Thine

by taking them presents on this sleigh of mine."

"*I* love them, dear Jesus, but not like You can,
for You are their Savior, and I'm but a man."
Then Santa's eyes filled up with tears.
They ran down his red cheeks to his snowy-white beard.

He told the Lord Jesus of his deepest fear
about boys' and girls' hearts at this time of year:
"So many, my Savior, believe in me but not You.
They see me as their Christmas, not knowing what's true."

"A nicely wrapped gift is their Christmas delight,
with hardly a thought of You coming that night.
Empty, so empty their Christmas will be,
if they don't think of You and just look for me."

"Oh, Jesus," said Santa, "You are the reason for the trees and the lights and the whole Christmas season!
I'm but a part of Christmastime fun.
You are the Christ child.

You're real. You're God's Son."

$\mathcal{T}$hen Santa stood up. He had a task now to do,
some rooftops to visit, a million or two.
So onward and upward and skyward away
flew the Christmastime reindeer
and a Santa who prayed.

O Holy Night

For unto you is born this
day in the city of
David, a Savior, which
is Christ the Lord.

—Luke 2:11

YAY! We love the true meaning of Christmas!

O come let us adore Him!

For God so loved the world so much that He gave His only Son so that anyone who believes in Him should not perish but have eternal life. John 3:16

(The Living Bible)

Acknowledgment

Julie Dinardo Jones

Thank you for your overwhelming encouragement and support.

About the Author

The author wrote this poem in 1988 for a children's church program. She has been encouraged to publish it for years. The birth of her granddaughter, however, was the turning point for finally doing so.

Her hope is that seeds of faith will be planted in hearts by the reading of this book as young minds turn their focus to God's greatest gift, Jesus.

CPSIA information can be obtained
at www.ICGtesting.com
Printed in the USA
LVHW071357191122
733281LV00008B/397